Class One Farmyard Fun

To Mrs Ivett and the pupils of Woburn
Lower School where the bull first raged.
J.J.

To my very special, long-suffering John,
with love x
L.C.

HODDER CHILDREN'S BOOKS
First published in Great Britain in 2017 by Hodder and Stoughton

Text copyright © Julia Jarman, 2017
Illustrations copyright © Lynne Chapman, 2017

A CIP catalogue record for this book is available from the British Library.

HB ISBN: 978 1 444 92715 3
PB ISBN: 978 1 444 92716 0

10 9 8 7 6 5 4 3 2 1

Printed and bound in China

MIX
Paper from
responsible sources
FSC® C104740
www.fsc.org

Hodder Children's Books
An imprint of Hachette Children's Group
Part of Hodder and Stoughton
Carmelite House
50 Victoria Embankment
London EC4Y 0DZ

An Hachette UK Company
www.hachette.co.uk
www.hachettechildrens.co.uk

Class One
Farmyard
Fun

JULIA JARMAN

Illustrated by
LYNNE CHAPMAN

Hodder
Children's
Books

When **Class One** went to **Fribbly Farm,**
they saw the farmer by the barn.
They saw a **goat** eating his coat

and a giggly **goose**
in a rowing boat.

But they didn't see. . .

...the bull!

BEWARE
OF THE
BULL

They **heard** Teacher say,
'Follow the code:
close all the gates, and
mind that load!'

They saw some **piglets** doing plops.

But they didn't see...

. . .the bull in a **strop**.

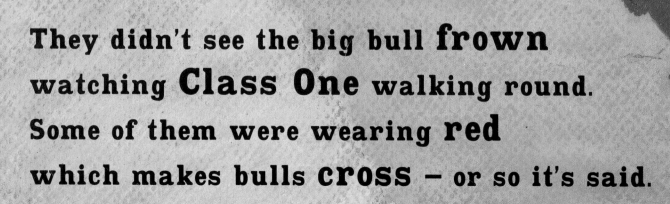

They didn't see the big bull **frown**
watching **Class One** walking round.
Some of them were wearing **red**
which makes bulls **cross** – or so it's said.

They saw a **lot** of woolly **sheep** and a **cock** on top of a **whiffy** muck heap.

But they **didn't** see...

. . .**huge** nostrils **flare**

and **puff out clouds** of steamy air.

They saw **ducks** dabbling in the lake

and **COWS** busy
making yummy **milkshakes**.

But they **didn't** see...

. . .the bull **paw** the ground,

then **charge**

at a gate and...

. . .knock it **down!**

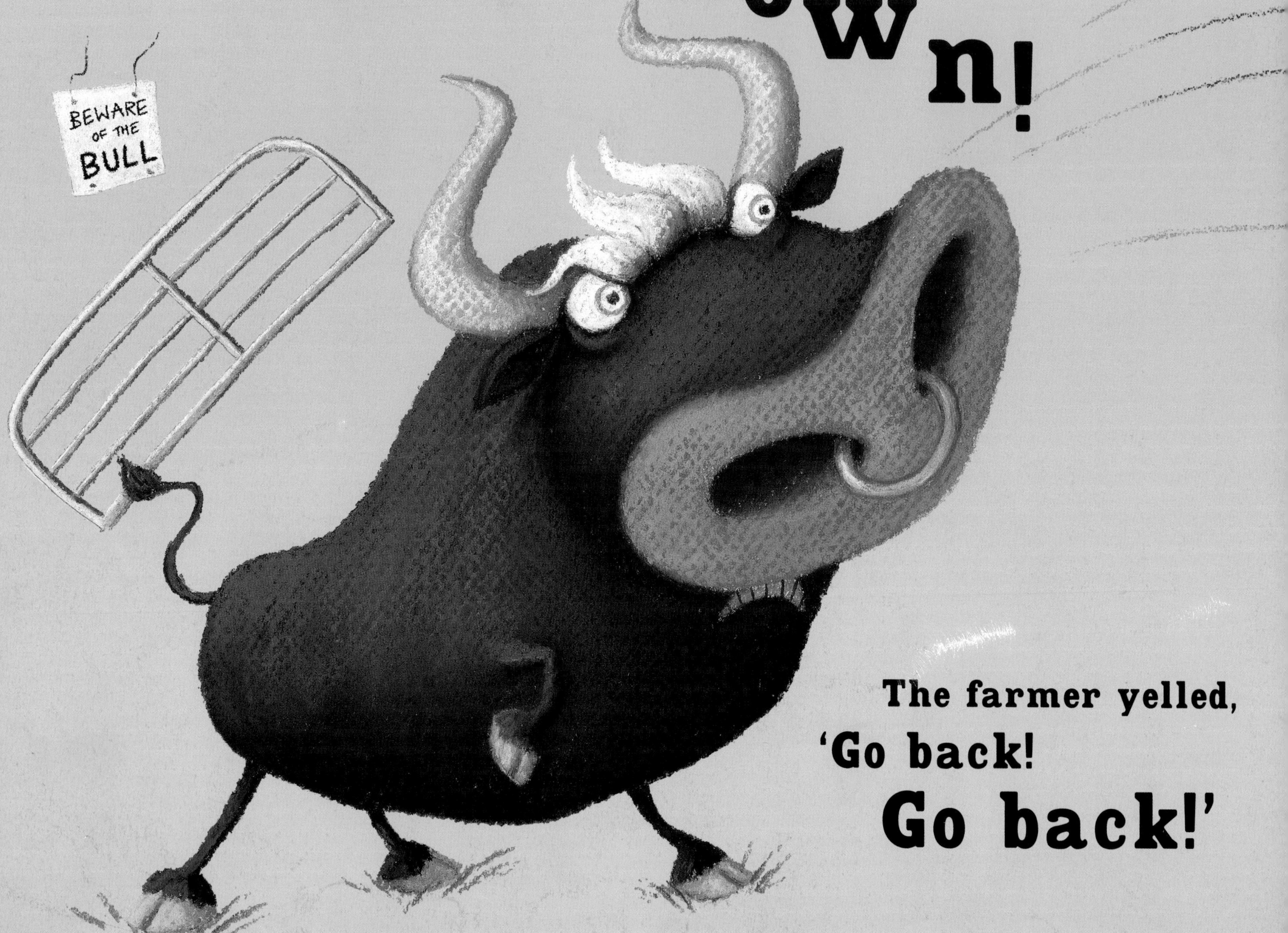

The farmer yelled,
'Go back!
Go back!'

But - **biff!** -

he **flew into**

a **prickly** haystack!

The bull

then

crept

along

the

lane

after Carol and Mary Jane.

He hid behind
a holly hedge,
so he could keep
an eye on Reg.

Then...

'**Miss!**' they cried.
'**It's ever so smelly!**'

But Miss was busy cleaning her wellies.

'**Look out!**' yelled Sam, but much too late. . .

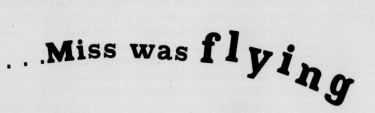

...Miss was **flying**

over the gate.

Please close the gate

Now the bull
went after Paul,

but – **phew!** –
he crashed into a wall.

Meanwhile Miss and a **duck** landed in the farmer's truck.

Miss hissed, '**Children**, hide in **here**! The bull is **waking up** I fear.'

She was right –
his eyelids
flickered –

enraged by
a pair of bright
red knickers.

But luckily
   Sam had a plan.
'Miss, **quick**, drive
   as **fast** as you can

past that washing and down the track.
With **luck** we'll get that **bad bull** back
in the field from where he came
and lock him **safely** up again.'

But could Miss do it?

Sam got the prop. . .

. . .and took the **pants** off that bull in a strop.

Waving them he yelled, 'Olé!
Catch us if you can! OK?'

The bull charged on
enraged by **red**
as **Miss** drove the truck
straight ahead.

Then suddenly the truck swerved right,

but the **bull** ran on out of sight. . .

. . .into the field
where Jamie and Jock
secured the gate with a
strong new lock.

So if your class goes
on a trip to a farm,
make sure **you** don't come to harm.

Wear green
or yellow,
purple or blue.

Just don't
wear **red**,
whatever
you do!